ROSCOE
JUNCTION

HOME

Swift smelled the gun oil.
He knew we were going hunting a week before we left.
He's what Pa calls a knowledgeable dog.

Ma says Pa and Swift were out hunting on the day I was born—and that I have wanted to go with them ever since.

This year I passed the gun course. This year Pa said, "Johnnie, get the dog. We're goin' huntin'."

All the first day I threw sticks for Swift, but he wouldn't chase them like he does at home.

"How come Swift won't fetch?" I asked Pa.

"Because he's workin' now," Pa said.

The second day Swift led us through thickets and streambeds.

"Do you think Swift will find us a bear?" I asked.

"He'll have to if we're to have enough food to get us through the winter," Pa answered.

The next day Swift led us up steep hills and down deep ravines.

"Swift ain't having much luck," I told Pa.

My father sighed and put down his gun.

"There's a lot of land out there," he said, "and very few bears. It ain't about luck. It's about figuring out the bear before the bear figures out you." Pa turned when Swift let out a bark.

A grizzly ran out of the brush.
Pa pushed me to the ground.
"Tuck your head!" he hollered as he
ran for his gun.
I did.
I heard the bear growl.
Then I heard something heavy hit a tree.
Swift went wild, snarling and barking
like I never heard him before.
"Swift—move!" Pa spit out.
I heard *click-click*.
He'd gotten to his gun.
BOOM
BOOM
Then I heard nothing.
I peeked out from under my arms.
The bear was gone.
"Pa!" I called.
My father was down.

Pa's leg was bent at a terrible angle.

"Gonna need your help," he whispered.

I nodded my head.

"Find a couple of straight branches. Strap my leg to them," he said.

I did.

"Get some brush and make a shelter under this tree."

I did.

"Now you and Swift go get help," Pa said.

"What if the bear comes back?" I asked.

Pa tapped his gun. "It might.

"Listen carefully," he said. "Find the shortcut through the forest and take it to the beaver pond. From there follow the runoff to Geezer's abandoned cabin. You got that?"

"Forest, pond, runoff, cabin," I repeated.

"Then find his old rowboat and get downstream to Roscoe Junction for help."

"Boat, river, Roscoe."

Pa looked at me with hard, unblinking eyes. "Keep your wits about you and, Johnnie, Swift knows this route. Listen to the dog."

Swift was already starting down the trail.

I felt mixed up about leaving Pa.
What if he was hurt worse than I thought?
I walked faster.
What if the bear came back for him?
I started to run.
What if the bear came after Swift and me?
I ran. I ran. I ran.
Until Swift dove under my feet and I
went down hard.
He'd stopped me from running off a cliff.
Keep your wits about you, Pa had said.
Swift knew—going too fast can be as bad
as going too slow.

Further on, Swift came to a tall tree. I thought he was going to leave his scent, but no, he just kept circling it.

"What is it?" I asked.

The dog looked up.

He'd seen Pa climb many a tree to get his bearings.

I grabbed a branch and pulled myself up.

Directly below us I saw the trail into the forest. It looked like an easy shortcut to the beaver pond.

Swift's hackles went up the moment he stepped into the forest. There were things in there that he didn't like. Things that smelled wet and musky. Things that rushed away when he ran up to the edge of the trail. Mile after mile there were things in the forest.

Swift's ears went straight. He turned his head and suddenly ran off the trail. I ran in after him, but I couldn't keep up.

I leaned on a tree but then sucked in my breath. From far away came the sound of a fight. One final bark rose above the others.

Swift.

Then the whole forest went quiet.

Checking my gun, I headed out again. But it wasn't long before every tree and every rock looked the same. By the time dusk came on, I was lost.

I took cover under a fallen tree. Swift would come. He had to come. The air turned cold and the forest felt close. I wondered if the forest felt as cold and close for Pa under that tree with his leg all busted up.

SNAP

Something was coming.

I peeked under the tree and there it was—standing in the clearing. Nose sniffing the air, the bear knew I was there.

I eased the gun barrel up and got him in my sight.

But the bear turned and narrowed its eyes at me. It froze me in my spot. When he moved toward me—

I couldn't fire the gun.

Swift burst out of the woods. I got a grip on myself.

"Boom," my head told my hand.

BOOM

The bear spun and went down on one knee.

"Go, Swift!" We turned tail and took off through the woods.

I knew I didn't get a good shot off. And I knew what Pa always said—that a wounded bear is the most dangerous bear. A wounded bear won't give you any warning. A wounded bear, Pa said, comes out of nowhere.

I ran behind Swift until a bright white light dusted the trail.

It was snowing outside the forest.

The beaver dam was straight ahead.

Swift didn't like the beaver
dam. But I didn't like the forest.
He carefully picked his way across the top.
I kept turning around, gun ready, watching for
the bear.
I should have done what Swift did and watched
my steps. My foot slipped and some logs kicked
out from under me. Loose wood, frozen mud and
I fell into the runoff below.

Icy water seeped into every stitch of my clothes. Swift was next to me in an instant. *Up.* He nudged me. *Up.*

My body started shaking from the cold. "We ain't gonna make it!" I cried.

Swift stopped nudging. He moved his head so close to mine that I could feel his breath. That's when I saw all the dried blood and matted hair. The fight hadn't gone well for Swift. He was hurt and worn-out too.

But nothing was going to stop him. He had a job to do. No time for tears. Time only to move on.

My frozen clothes crackled as I got up and followed him down the streambed to the tundra land.

It was slow going through the tundra. Sometimes the frozen ground held up, other times it fell through, throwing me over the hay heads. At first my frozen feet were itchy. Then they began to hurt. I chased away the pain by telling myself I was walking on soft summer grass.

"Summer grass," I kept saying to myself, "summer grass."

But the next time I fell, I thought I actually was on summer grass, and it felt so good that I wanted to lie in that grass forever.

I closed my eyes.

I thought I heard Swift barking far away. Closer, I heard him again.

"It's . . . 's . . . 's-okay, S-Swift-t-t-t." I couldn't stop shaking.
But he wouldn't stop until I looked up.
He'd found Geezer's cabin.

Inside, Swift sniffed every corner of the cabin. I tried to start a fire, but all my matches were wet. I threw them down and fell to the floor. *Summer grass.*

Suddenly Swift jumped on me.

"G-g-go a-a-away," I told him, still shaking.

But he wouldn't stop. He grabbed hold of my pant leg and shook.

"No!" I kicked at him.

Swift turned toward the door and growled.

The griz was outside, weaving and insane. If it got into the cabin, we'd be trapped.

Swift leaped out the door. I grabbed the gun.

The grizzly threw my dog. Swift's breath blew out of him as he hit the ground. He was slow getting up. The bear lurched forward and filled up the doorway. Its eyes looked at me, trying to hold me still. But he wouldn't have me this time. This time—

BOOM

This time I dispatched the bear.

I had to.

Swift jumped aside as the griz fell backward into the snow.

My dog carefully approached the griz, sniffed it and jumped back. Then cautiously he walked back and pawed at the bear. One more sniff and Swift stepped aside.

That bear wasn't going to trouble anyone anymore.

"C'mon, Swift," I said. We had to get Geezer's boat.

Geezer's rowboat was frozen to the shoreline. I rocked it free.
But I'd have to get into the river and break my way out to the
running water. My body tightened as I stepped in.

"Pa!" I said each time I kicked at the ice.

"Pa!" I said each time I pounded with my hands.

My whole body was numb when we made it to running water.

After that, I don't know how I got into the boat.

After that, I just remember the dreaming.

I dreamed.

I dreamed that the boat was being tossed around on chattering white teeth.

I dreamed the bear was sneaking up on Pa, and I jumped awake, wide-eyed and scared for him. Then I dreamed that the frozen stiffness in my clothing softened, as snow turned to sleet and sleet turned to rain.

And always, anytime my eyes opened, Swift was there, giving up his warmth to me.

I dreamed the water sounded like voices, as running water will. Then I felt Swift stir, jamming his legs into me to stand up and look around. His whole body began to shake and a low whine grew up from deep inside him.

I dreamed that voices surrounded the boat.

The voices became real.

We'd made it to Roscoe Junction.

Nothing seemed real until they asked me about Pa.

"Bear broke his leg. He's above the beaver pond, on Tarhook Ridge."

Until they asked me how I made it back.

"Kept my wits about me."

Until they asked me if there was anything else they needed to know.

And I pointed to my dog, already on his way.

"Listen to Swift. He's a knowledgeable dog."

For Larry, Kathy, Grace and Robert Lake

AUTHOR'S NOTE

Until recently, people could still stake a claim to homestead land in Alaska. To homestead, one had to choose up to forty acres of land and then stake it and file for it. Within five years a habitable shelter had to be built on the surveyed land.

For the most part, homesteaders live off the land. They raise vegetables during the short growing season. In fall, they must hunt for their own meat or they might not have enough food to eat through the long Alaskan winter.

To create the book *Swift*, I moved in with a homesteading family near Healy, Alaska. Many other homesteaders stopped by to visit. As I listened to their various conversations and stories, I wrote many words in my sketchbook. I drew many pictures while walking in the wilderness.

While I was there, an injured bear was seen wandering in the area. I joined the men as they went out to find the bear. It was a tense and exciting experience. I learned a lot about just how difficult and dangerous homesteading can be.

Many people who have staked claims are still living as homesteaders in Alaska. The comforts that many of us take for granted are far away from them. They deserve a lot of respect. In them, the spirit of adventure still lives on.

Patricia Lee Gauch, Editor

PHILOMEL BOOKS

A division of Penguin Young Readers Group.
Published by The Penguin Group.
Penguin Group (USA) Inc., 375 Hudson Street, New York, NY 10014, U.S.A.
Penguin Group (Canada), 90 Eglinton Avenue East, Suite 700, Toronto, Ontario, Canada M4P 2Y3
(a division of Pearson Penguin Canada Inc.).
Penguin Books Ltd, 80 Strand, London WC2R 0RL, England.
Penguin Ireland, 25 St. Stephen's Green, Dublin 2, Ireland (a division of Penguin Books Ltd).
Penguin Group (Australia), 250 Camberwell Road, Camberwell, Victoria 3124, Australia
(a division of Pearson Australia Group Pty Ltd).
Penguin Books India Pvt Ltd, 11 Community Centre, Panchsheel Park, New Delhi - 110 017, India.
Penguin Group (NZ), 67 Apollo Drive, Mairangi Bay, Auckland 1311, New Zealand
(a division of Pearson New Zealand Ltd).
Penguin Books (South Africa) (Pty) Ltd, 24 Sturdee Avenue, Rosebank, Johannesburg 2196, South Africa.
Penguin Books Ltd, Registered Offices: 80 Strand, London WC2R 0RL, England.

Published simultaneously in Canada.
Manufactured in China by South China Printing Co. Ltd.
Design by Semadar Megged.   The artist used oil paint to create the illustrations for this book.
The text is set in 14-Point Meridien Medium.
Library of Congress Cataloging-in-Publication Data

ISBN 978-0-399-23383-8
1 3 5 7 9 10 8 6 4 2
First Impression

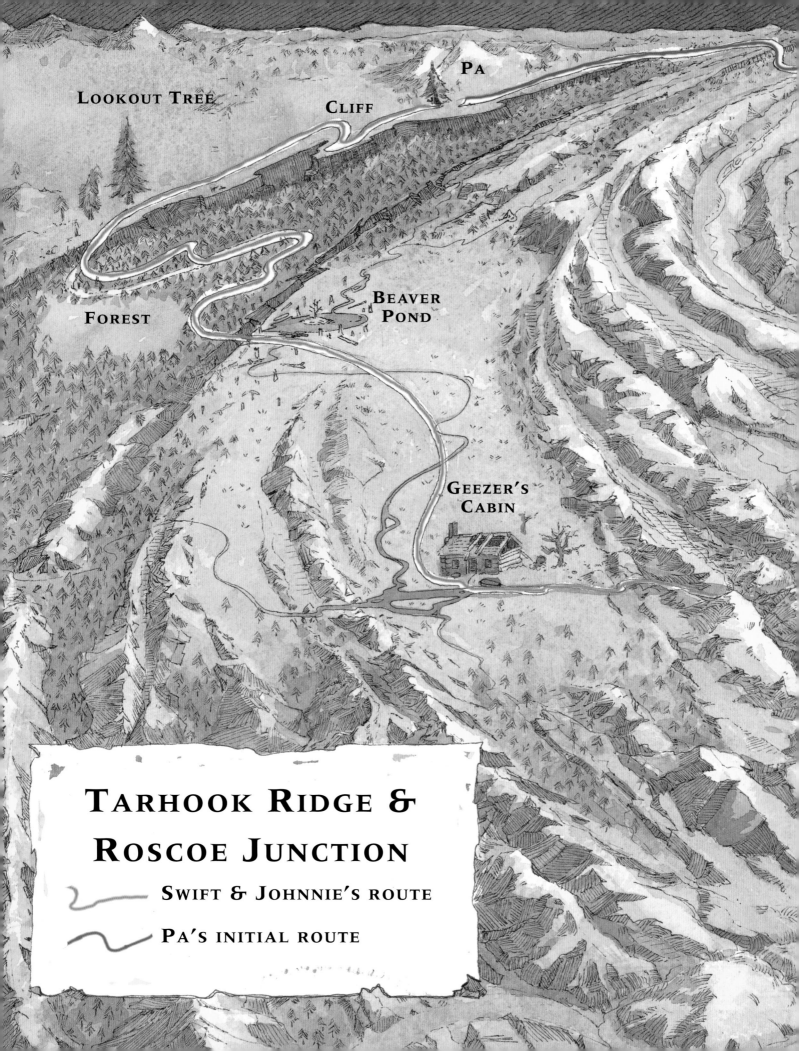

LOOKOUT TREE

PA

CLIFF

FOREST

BEAVER POND

GEEZER'S CABIN

TARHOOK RIDGE & ROSCOE JUNCTION

SWIFT & JOHNNIE'S ROUTE

PA'S INITIAL ROUTE